*For my father, with love.*

www.enchantedlionbooks.com

First American edition published in 2015 by Enchanted Lion Books,
351 Van Brunt Street, Brooklyn, NY 11231
Copyright © 2015 by Enchanted Lion books for the English-language translation
Originally published in France in 2002 as *Scritch scratch dip clapote!*
Text and illustrations by Kitty Crowther
Translated from the French by Claudia Zoe Bedrick
Copyright © 2002 by l'école des loisirs, Paris
All rights reserved under International and Pan-American Copyright Conventions
A CIP record is on file with the Library of Congress
ISBN 978-1-59270-179-7
Printed in China by RR Donnelley Asia Printing Solutions Limited Company
First edition 2015

10 9 8 7 6 5 4 3 2 1

# Kitty Crowther

# Scritch Scratch Scraww Plop!

ENCHANTED LION BOOKS

NEW YORK

Every evening, the sun sets over the pond.
And every evening, Jeremy feels afraid.

"Time for bed, my little frog," says Mom.

Jeremy checks that the front door is tightly shut.

Then he hops through the water after his mom.

As long as she is there, Jeremy feels happy.

In the bathroom,
Jeremy washes his hands
and face.

Mom listens
as he brushes his teeth.

Then he puts his pajamas
on all by himself
and Mom buttons him up.

"One last pee-pee
and then to bed!"
Mom sings out.

She knows her little frog is afraid of the dark.
"Daddy is coming to read you a wonderful bedtime story."

Daddy is here! Jeremy snuggles up close.
He wishes he could stay like this forever!

"Sweet dreams, my little froggy.
Don't be afraid. I'm right in the next room.
I'll get Mama for your goodnight kiss."
Dad gives Jeremy a kiss and goes for Mom.

"Mama, I want a hug!"

"And a kiss."

"Another hug."

"And a kiss."
"All right, my
little green bundle...

It's time for sleep. I'll leave
the light on in the hallway.

You'll be as snug
as a little mouse."

"I'm all alone in my room," thinks Jeremy.

"All alone in my bed.

All alone in my heart!"

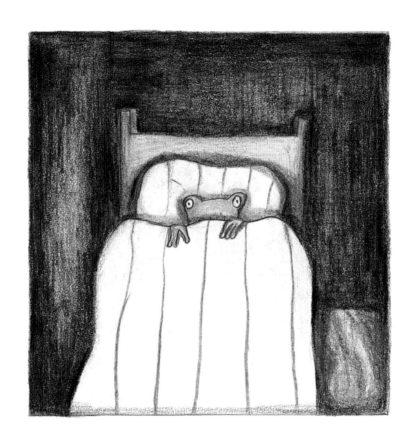

I think I hear a noise...

**Who is going**
**"scritch scratch scraww plop"**
**under my bed?**

Is it a water monster?

A feathered snake?

Maybe it's a swamp skeleton?

Jeremy is so afraid his tummy hurts.

He hurries to his parents' bedroom.

"Daddy, Daddy!" whispers Jeremy.
"Wake up! There's something going
scritch scratch scraww plop under my bed."
Dad opens one eye.
"Scritch scratch scraww plop?" he sighs.

"Oh, little froggy,

those are only the sounds of the night.

Let's tuck you back into bed."

"Now, go to sleep, Jeremy," says Dad.
He gently closes his son's eyes with his fingers.
"You'll see. The next time you open your eyes,
it will be morning."

**But it's not morning at all!**
**And Scritch scratch scraww plop is still there.**

Once more, Jeremy runs to his parents' bedroom.
"Scritch scratch scraww plop is still there."

"Come on, little one, it's late.
There's no Scritch scratch skraww plop in your room.
At this hour, even that's gone to sleep,"
grumbles Dad.

Once again, Jeremy feels alone.

Awfully alone.

**Trembling, he slips quietly into the hall.**

"Mommy, I'm frightened!"
Mom wakes up and takes Jeremy in her arms.

He climbs into his parents' bed.

At last, he can sleep.

But poor Dad can't fall asleep next to the wriggly Jeremy.
Exhausted, he goes down the hall...

and gets into Jeremy's little bed,

where he falls right to sleep.

But a "scritch scratch scraww plop"

startles him awake.

"What on earth is that?"

He goes to wake Jeremy.
"Come on," Dad whispers.
"Let's go see what's making that
scritch scratch scraww plop."

Dad and Jeremy swim through the darkness
towards a great big lily pad.

In the stillness of the night,
they hear "scritch scratch scraww plop."

Scritch scratch! A mole digs a hole to her home.

Scraww! A bird calls into the night.

Plop! A silver fish leaps out of the water
and dives back in.

Jeremy looks out into the night and smiles.

"You know what, Dad?
I don't think I'm scared of the dark anymore."

And there on the lily pad, they drift
off to sleep, lulled by the water
and the scritch...scratch...scraww...plop.